Goldie and the THREE HARES

By Margie Palatini   Illustrated by Jack E. Davis

 KATHERINE TEGEN BOOKS
An Imprint of HarperCollins Publishers

6/11

Katherine Tegen Books is an imprint of HarperCollins Publishers.

Goldie and the Three Hares
Text copyright © 2011 by Margie Palatini
Illustrations copyright © 2011 by Jack E. Davis

Library of Congress Cataloging-in-Publication Data
Palatini, Margie.
Goldie and the three hares / by Margie Palatini ; illustrated by Jack E. Davis. — 1st ed.
p. cm.
Summary: When Goldilocks, running from the three bears, falls down a rabbit hole and hurts her
foot, a family of hares tries to help, but she proves to be a very loud, demanding, and tenacious guest.
ISBN 978-0-06-125314-0 (trade bdg.) — ISBN 978-0-06-125315-7 (lib. bdg.)
[1. Hospitality—Fiction. 2. Behavior—Fiction. 3. Hares—Fiction. 4. Characters in literature—Fiction.
5. Humorous stories.] I. Davis, Jack E., ill. II. Title.
PZ7.P1755Gmm   2010   2008036910   [E]—dc22   CIP   AC

Typography by Rachel Zegar
11 12 13   LP/CW   10 9 8 7 6 5 4 3 2

First Edition

For my Big "Baby Bunny"

—M.P.

For Thomas Curt Davis

—J.E.D.

Papa Hare, Mama Hare, and Little Baby Hare
(also known as Bunny) were enjoying a quiet, peaceful, lovely day at
home down their rabbit hole.

THUMP. BUMP. KABOOM. KABOOM. KABOOM!

That was not quiet. Or peaceful.

"Get me outta here!"

And that didn't sound lovely.

"What was that?" said Papa and Mama.

Quick to the door ran Bunny. "A foot!" he cried, peeking through the tiny window. "A big little foot that belongs to a big little girl who fell down our rabbit hole and landed *splat* on our door stoop!"

"I said, get me outta here!"

The Hares hopped right over to help.
"What happened?" asked Papa Hare.
"How did you get here?" asked Mama Hare.
"Who are you?" asked Bunny.

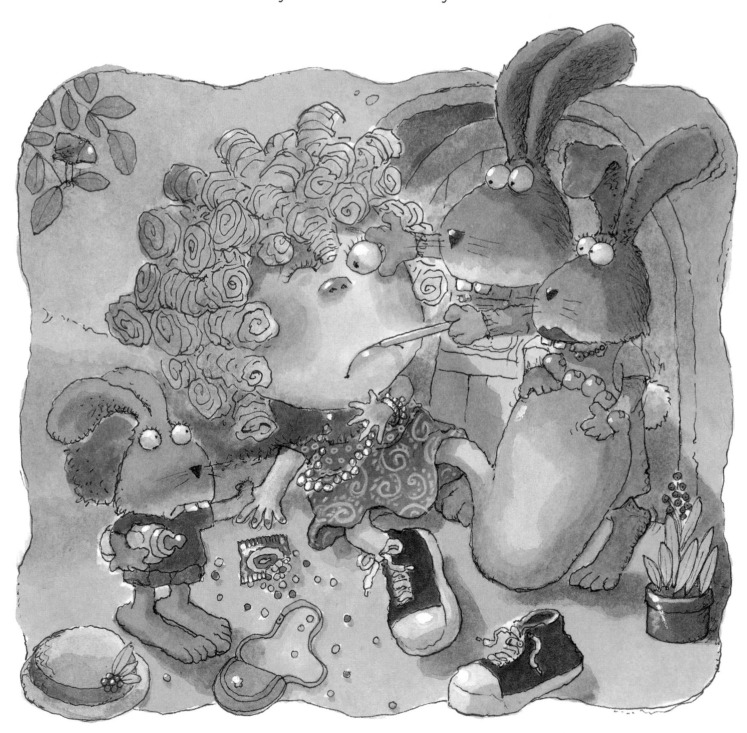

"Questions. Questions. Questions! Can't you see this head of hair? I'm Goldilocks. I was chased through the woods by three bears, I fell down your rabbit hole—and let me tell you, that first step is a lulu—and now my little foot is big and swollen and I can't get out."

Papa, Mama, and Little Baby Hare watched the big little
foot grow bigger by the minute.

There was just no way now to get *you-know-who* up and
out of the rabbit hole with that fat foot swelling.

Well, they all couldn't just stay there watching the foot,
so the three Hares helped the big little girl into their house.

"Watch that tootsie! Don't muss the hair!"

The three Hares huffed and puffed and carried her to Papa Hare's chair.

"Wait! Stop! This chair looks too hard."

They huffed and puffed and carried her to Mama Hare's chair.

"Wait! Stop! This chair looks too soft."

They huffed and puffed and stared at Baby Hare's chair.

"Don't even go there! I'll take the couch!"

Which she did. With both feet up on the cushions.
"Now, this is just right."
(Not really. Mama didn't allow shoes on the sofa.)
But there she sat. All settled in. Big shoe and all.

"I told you to fix that lulu of a first step," muttered
Mama to Papa.

So, with the big little girl all comfy-cozy on the sofa, Bunny sat down to read a book, Mama picked up her knitting, and Papa went to see about that lulu of a first step.

"Hey! I need a pillow here! Now! Quick like a bunny—and remember, not too hard. Not too soft. Just right . . . And get one for my foot too."

And with the big little girl even more settled in, with
three pillows and her shoe up on the sofa, Bunny sat
down to read his book, Mama went back to her knitting,
and Papa went to fix that lulu of a first step.

"Uh . . . ? Haven't we forgotten something here? Like a blanket? I need a blanket!"

"Too scratchy. Too itchy. Too big. Too little. Too hot. Way too skimpy! Actually, I prefer cashmere. And somebody turn up the heat, will you?"

"Okay, where's the clicker? Who's got the remote? . . .
What? No cable? You—Baby Bunny Ears—go stand by
the TV so I can get a better picture."

"Perfect! Don't move a muscle!"

"Oh dear," said Mama. "I don't believe
Bunny can stay like that for very long."

Luckily for the Hares, the big little girl felt so comfy-cozy and the TV program was so long and boring, she fell sound asleep.

Mama sighed. "How are we ever going to get her to leave?"

Papa came up with a marvelous plan.

"When *you-know-who* wakes up, she's going to be hungry. We're rabbits! All we have to eat are vegetables. Give her some carrots, spinach, and a little bit of cabbage and she'll be running for the door—big foot and all—before we know it."

Sure enough, when the big little girl awoke, her tummy was growling.
"I'm starving here! Bring on the snacks!"

Mama Hare came from the kitchen carrying a cup of carrot
juice, two spinach pies, and five steamed Brussels sprouts.
The three Hares tried their very best not to grin big,
broad, toothy grins. Their plan was working perfectly. Then
the big little girl picked up a sprout.

"I love veggies! Toss me some arugula!"
The big little girl not only had all their pillows, best blankets, and her shoe up on the sofa, but now she was eating them out of house, home, and every vegetable. Including the carrot tops.

Papa sighed. "Now what?"

Mama had a dandy idea. "We'll invite the neighbors for a visit."

With the Hare house being so small, the neighbors being so
many, and *you-know-who* being so large, certainly the big little girl
would not want to stay where it was so cramped and crowded.

"Company? I *love* parties! Which one of
you bunnies brought the artichoke dip?"

This called for desperate measures.

It was time to bring in Sherman.

No one cleared a room quite like he did.

And when Sherman showed, sure enough, everyone made
a swift beeline for the door. Except for, well . . .

You-know-who.

"This stinks," said Little Baby Hare.

"I don't understand it," said Mama Hare, holding her nose.

"How can she still be here?" wondered Papa with his eyes smarting.

"Aachoo! Aachoo! I can't breave. My nuz is all stuffy and I can't smell a ting. I think I caud a code from dis drafty rabbit hole. I gotta get to bed and stay dare till I get all bedder!"

Baby Hare saw the big little girl eyeing his "just right" little bed.

"I've had it!" said Bunny, speed-dialing. "I'm calling—the Bears."

"DA BEARS?"

"Uh. Gotta go. Good-bye. So long. See you.
Arrivederci, rabbits!"

The big little girl with the big swollen foot scooted
out of the Hare house without even an aachoo and
ran up the rabbit hole, past that lulu of a first step.
And the three Hares went back to enjoying a quiet,
peaceful, lovely day at home in their rabbit hole.

THUMP. BUMP. KABOOM. KABOOM. KABOOM!

Bunny peeked through the tiny window.
"Oh no! It's another big little foot that belongs to another big little girl who fell down our rabbit hole and landed *splat* on our door stoop!"

"Pardon me.
I say, has anyone seen a white rabbit lately?"

"I have *got* to fix that lulu of a first step."